TRICERATOPS GETS LOST

by Dawn Bentley

Illustrated by Karen Carr

Book copyright © 2003 Trudy Corporation
and the Smithsonian Institution, Washington DC 20560

Published by Soundprints Division of Trudy Corporation, Norwalk, Connecticut.

Book design: Marcin D. Pilchowski
Editor: Laura Gates Galvin
Editorial assistance: Chelsea Shriver

First Edition 2003
10 9 8 7 6 5 4 3 2 1
Printed in China

Acknowledgements:
    Our very special thanks to Dr. Brett-Surman of the Smithsonian Institution's National Museum of Natural History.
    Soundprints would like to thank Ellen Nanney and Katie Mann of the Smithsonian Institution for their help in the creation of the book.

Library of Congress Cataloging-in-Publication Data

 Bentley, Dawn
     Triceratops gets lost / by Dawn Bentley ; illustrated by Karen Carr.
  p. cm.
 Summary: A young triceratops becomes separated from his heard and encounters a Tyrannosaurus rex.
   ISBN 1-59249-165-0 (HC) – ISBN 1-59249-166-9 (pbk.) – ISBN 1-59249-167-7 (micro)
   [1. Triceratops—Fiction. 2. Dinosaurs—Fiction.] I. Carr, Karen, 1960- ill. II. Title

PZ7.B447494Tr 2003
[E]—dc21
                                                                                          2003050358

TRICERATOPS GETS LOST

by Dawn Bentley

Illustrated by Karen Carr

Soundprints
Where Children Discover...

A lush valley comes to life in the warm glow of the morning sun. Gingko trees sway in the gentle breeze. It's the perfect day for a young Triceratops and his herd to look for their favorite plants to eat.

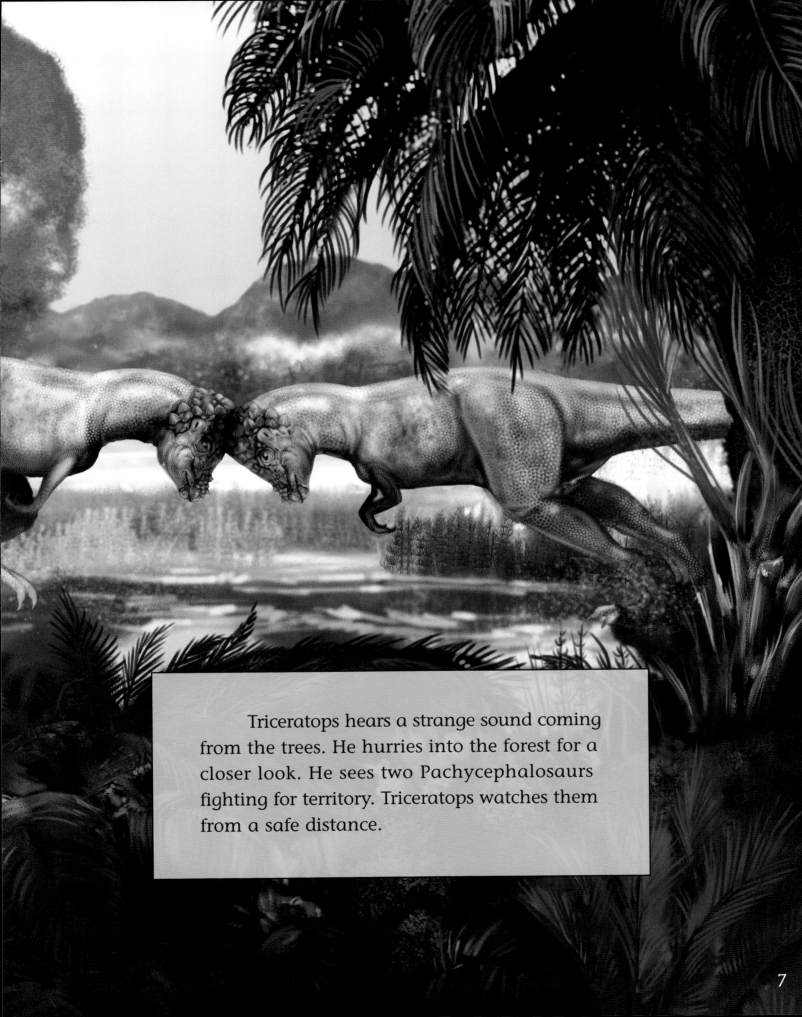

Triceratops hears a strange sound coming from the trees. He hurries into the forest for a closer look. He sees two Pachycephalosaurs fighting for territory. Triceratops watches them from a safe distance.

Sun shines through the trees, scattering light on the ferns below. Triceratops loves to eat ferns! He uses his razor-sharp beak to cut through a tough stem. His strong jaw and perfectly designed teeth crush the plant into easy-to-swallow pieces.

Beginning to feel full, Triceratops looks up from his meal and realizes the other members of his group are not in the forest with him. He doesn't feel safe alone. He must find his herd!

Cautiously, he approaches a clearing. He hears loud squawking sounds from above. He looks up and sees giant Quetzalcoatlus gliding down toward him in a great spiraling circle. He quickly runs for cover. When he looks back, he sees the Quetzalcoatlus are much more interested in something they see on the ground.

Triceratops approaches a sparkling stream that runs through the lush valley. Frogs, snakes and turtles line the shore. Triceratops plods through the muddy banks into the shallow water. In the distance, he sees a Parasaurolophus eating reeds, but Triceratops' group is still nowhere in sight!

15

Triceratops is tired of walking. He finds a shady place to rest. He is about to fall asleep when suddenly a loud thumping noise disrupts the peaceful chatter of birds. Animals cry out in alarm and scatter into the bushes to hide.

The sound of crunching footsteps grows louder and louder, closer and closer—then stops. Triceratops looks around at the rustling leaves above. Two piercing eyes stare down at him. It's Tyrannosaurus rex, one of the fiercest dinosaurs in all the land!

The Tyrannosaurus rex continues to stare down at Triceratops. Her long tail sticks straight out behind her, perfectly balancing her body and huge head. The Tyrannosaurus rex is hungry, and Triceratops would make a very tasty meal!

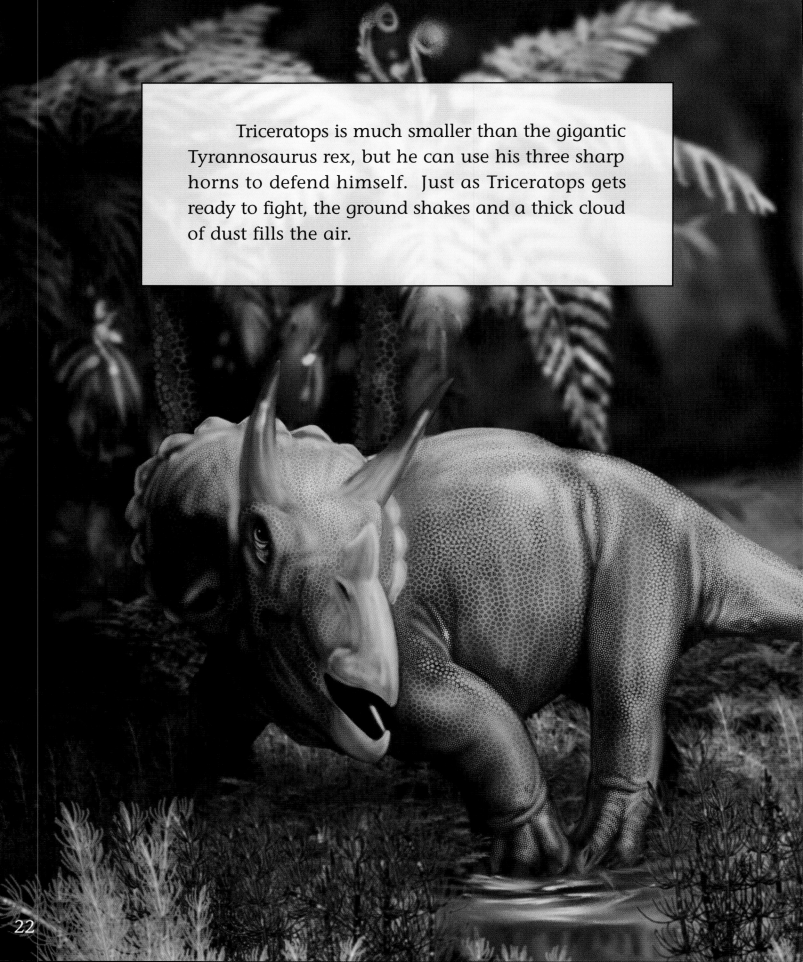

Triceratops is much smaller than the gigantic Tyrannosaurus rex, but he can use his three sharp horns to defend himself. Just as Triceratops gets ready to fight, the ground shakes and a thick cloud of dust fills the air.

Emerging from the dust is Triceratops' herd! They move in closer. They are ready to help Triceratops. There is no way the Tyrannosaurus rex can win this battle. Defeated, she stomps away.

It has been a long day. Triceratops feels safe now that he is finally back with his group, but all the activity has made him hungry! He huddles close to his herd, and together they return to the forest in search of plants to eat.

ABOUT THE TRICERATOPS
(try-SAIR-uh-tops)

Triceratops hasn't lived on earth since the Late Cretaceous period, which was about 65 million years ago. But paleontologists (pay-lee-uhn-TAH-lih-jists), people who study dinosaur fossils, have learned quite a bit about them by studying their bones.

Triceratops means "three-horned face." All Triceratops had three horns.

Triceratops were the largest and heaviest of the horned dinosaurs. They weighed about 11 tons and were nearly 30 feet long! Their big horns and bony neck shields would scare off some enemies and protect them from others.

These plant eaters had strong, sharp beaks that helped them bite through thick stems and branches.

▲ **Pachycephalosaur**

▲ **Parasaurolophus**

▲ **Dragonfly**

▲ **Turtles**

▲ Tyrannosaurus rex

▲ Frog

PICTORIAL GLOSSARY

▲ Triceratops

▲ Quetzalcoatlus